LITTLE FINGERLING

To my granddaughter Melissa, with love
and in memory of E.C.

M.H.

For Nanny, my wonderful
travelling grandmother

B.C.

Special thanks to Hugh Wylie and Jack Howard of the Far Eastern
Library at The Royal Ontario Museum for their kind assistance and
interest in this book.

Kids Can Press Ltd. gratefully acknowledges the
assistance of the Canada Council and the Ontario Arts
Council in the production of this book.

Canadian Cataloguing in Publication Data

Hughes, Monica, 1925–
    Little fingerling

ISBN 0-921103-78-6

I. Clark, Brenda.   II. Title

PS8565.U43L58 1989   jC813'.54   C88-095220-2
PZ7.H83Li 1989

Kids Can Press Ltd.
585 ½ Bloor Street West
Toronto, Ontario Canada M6G 1K5

Printed and bound in Hong Kong

89 0 9 8 7 6 5 4 3 2

LITTLE FINGERLING

a Japanese folk tale retold by
MONICA HUGHES
illustrated by
BRENDA CLARK

Kids Can Press Ltd.
TORONTO

ONCE upon a time, in old Japan, there lived a childless couple. Every year they prayed at the local shrine that they might have a child.

"Even a little child, no bigger than the tip of my finger," the wife begged.

At last their prayer was answered and a son was born to them. He was indeed very tiny, but they were happy and called him Issun Boshi, Little Fingerling.

By the time he was a year old, he was as long as his mother's thumb. By the time he was ten, he was as tall as his father's forefinger.

He grew up happy and resourceful, helping his mother in the house by preparing vegetables, and his father on the farm by picking weeds and gathering stray grains of rice.

But when he was fifteen years old, and the height of his father's longest finger, he said to himself, "I am a grown man and I have seen nothing of the world but my mother's charcoal stove and my father's plough."

He bowed to his parents. "Honoured Father, honoured Mother, you have given me a home for fifteen years. You have fed me, clothed me, taught me all you know. Now it is time for me to go into the world and make my own way."

His mother and father looked sadly at each other and thought, "How can our Little Fingerling make his way in the world? He will be trampled to death beneath the feet of the crowd." They begged him not to leave the safety of their home, but Issun Boshi was determined to seek his fortune.

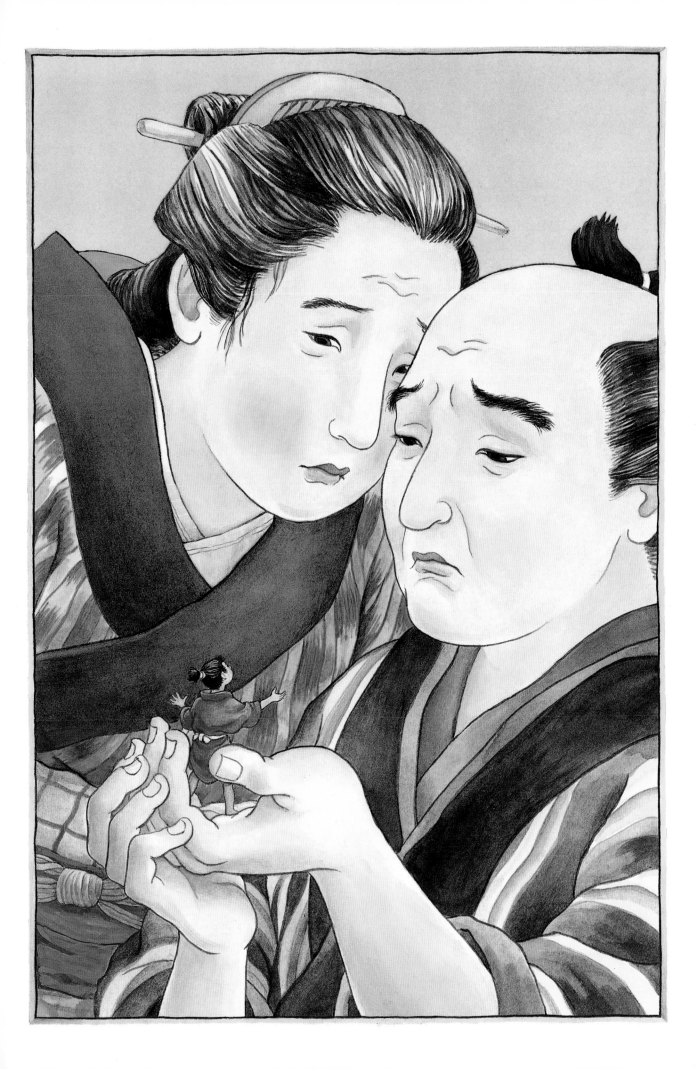

So his mother made him a fine travelling costume from a scrap of brocade and, out of a hollow straw, his father fashioned a scabbard for his sword, which was one of his mother's sewing needles. They also gave him their best lacquer rice bowl and a pair of fine chopsticks.

Issun Boshi bowed respectfully to his parents and set off down the road with his sword stuck in his sash, his chopsticks under one arm and his rice bowl over his head to keep his fine clothes dry, as it was raining.

Going around the puddles, which were too deep for him to wade through, he trudged down the path that led from the farm to the road that would take him to Kyoto. His small legs got very tired and, by the time the straw thatch of his parents' house was out of sight, he was beginning to wonder if he had made a wise choice.

But he kept walking. "I will go to Kyoto and make my way in the world," he told himself.

Some time later, he came to a stream crossing the road. "Water flows faster than my legs can trot," thought Issun Boshi. Quickly he put the rice bowl upon the water, stepped in and began to paddle with one of his chopsticks.

The little stream joined a river. The river became
wide and deep. Still Issun Boshi paddled on, until at
last he saw the golden tiles and thatched roofs of the
city of Kyoto.

"That wasn't too bad," he said as he jumped ashore and pulled his rice bowl after him. "Now where shall I go to look for work?" Following the crowds along the streets, he soon found himself in a marketplace. The stalls were piled with rice and fruit, with silks and lacquerware, with pots and chests and kimonos.

The crowds were so thick that Issun Boshi was in danger of being squashed under a foot or a barrel. In the end, he climbed up the cloth covering a stall that sold hairpins, combs and useful boxes, turned his rice bowl over and sat on it to catch his breath.

"Oh, see the little man!" In a minute there was a crowd around the stall.

The owner said craftily, "Good people, if you wish to see this fine and unusual sight, the least you can do is to buy some of my poor merchandise."

Everyone laughed and agreed that it was only fair. Before long, the stall owner's table was empty and his pouch was filled with coins.

"What luck brought you to me today?" he asked. "What is your name, if I may ask? And where are you from?"

Issun Boshi explained that he had come to Kyoto to make his way in the world.

"Then you need look no further. Come, join my humble household. You will have a comfortable bed and a full rice bowl. All I ask in return is that you sit on my table during working hours."

"Thank you, honoured sir." Issun Boshi stood up and bowed. "But it would not suit me at all to sit idly by. I know that the suit my mother made for me is very fine, as are my sword and scabbard, but they are not worthy of so much comment."

"Then help me with my work, if you wish. Your small fingers will decorate my combs most gracefully. Alas, the man who paints them is old and nearly blind."

So Issun Boshi agreed to work with the stall owner, filling in fine lines with gold lacquer on boxes and combs. In a few months, the stall owner's reputation had spread far and wide.

One day the wife of a nobleman came by, seeking combs for her only daughter's hair. She was fascinated by the sight of Issun Boshi sitting on top of the table, painting the finest imaginable designs in gold on a lacquered comb with a tiny mousehair brush.

"Honoured sir," she said. "Would you consider joining my household?"

"Will you permit me to leave?" Little Fingerling asked the stall owner. "You have kept your bargain. My bed is soft and my rice bowl is always full. Yet I crave a change."

The stall owner sighed. "I shall miss your skillful fingers, but leave if you must. You will go farther with a noble family than with a humble seller of boxes and combs."

Issun Boshi bowed deeply to the stall owner and his wife and hopped into the basket that the servant of the noblewoman carried.

In the house of the nobleman he learned to read and write, to fight with a sword and to dance, all the things that the children of the house learned.

They quickly grew very fond of him, especially the nobleman's daughter, whose name was Plum Blossom.

One day Plum Blossom wished to visit the temple of Kanzeon, the Goddess of Mercy. She wished to ask Kanzeon for help, for in spite of herself she had fallen in love with Issun Boshi.

"But how can I give my heart to a person who is smaller than my hand?" she asked herself. "Yet he is so brave and handsome that my knees shake whenever I see him."

"You cannot go to the shrine now, Plum Blossom," her mother said. "I am busy and the servants are all making rice cakes for the festival."

"I will go with you, honoured daughter of my mistress," exclaimed Issun Boshi, bowing very deeply. "I will protect you with my life." For Issun Boshi was secretly in love with Plum Blossom.

The family and servants all hid their smiles politely behind their hands at the idea of Issun Boshi escorting Plum Blossom, but she could not bear to hurt his feelings. "Thank you, Issun Boshi. I know I will be safe with you."

They set off along the cobbled streets that led from their house to the temple of Kanzeon. Suddenly a shadow fell across them and, with a horrible cry, two giant demons barred their way. These evil spirits were blue all over, with horns on their heads and three eyes. One of them swung a huge mallet.

They reached out hungrily towards the beautiful Plum Blossom, who fell to the ground in a swoon. At once Issun Boshi pulled his needle sword from its straw scabbard and leapt nimbly about, slashing at their greedy hands. But there were two of them and only one Issun Boshi, who was far smaller than their littlest fingers. At length one of them managed to grab him between finger and thumb.

Little Fingerling wriggled mightily, but the giant's grasp around his waist was too tight. He was lifted high into the air and popped into the giant's mouth.

It was very dark inside the giant's stomach and his huge heart thumped terribly. Only a little light appeared whenever he opened his mouth to roar.

"I must save Plum Blossom," Issun Boshi said to himself and, stabbing his sword into the giant's gullet, he pulled himself up. He stabbed and pulled until at last he was standing on the giant's tongue. Roaring with pain, the giant spat him out.

Issun Boshi tumbled to the ground, deafened by the giant's roar and dazed by his fall. While he was still stunned, the second giant picked him up and held him close to his face to look at him.

Quickly Issun Boshi stabbed the giant in one of his three great eyes and, with a terrible shriek, both demons vanished. Again poor Little Fingerling fell to the ground.

"What a terrible fall! Oh, honoured friend, are you still alive?"

Issun Boshi got to his feet and shook himself. "I am unharmed. But, honoured daughter of my mistress, how are you?"

"Thanks to your bravery, I am unhurt, dear Issun Boshi."

They both blushed and turned away from each other.

"See what the demons dropped in their hurry to be gone," Plum Blossom exclaimed. "I believe it is a lucky mallet, such as the one Daikoku, the God of Wealth and Good Fortune, carries. They say that when struck upon the ground it will grant your wish."

"Alas, it is too heavy for me," Little Fingerling said sadly.

"Allow me to strike it for you. What is your wish?"

Issun Boshi looked down and could say nothing, for he knew that it was impossible that he could ever marry Plum Blossom.

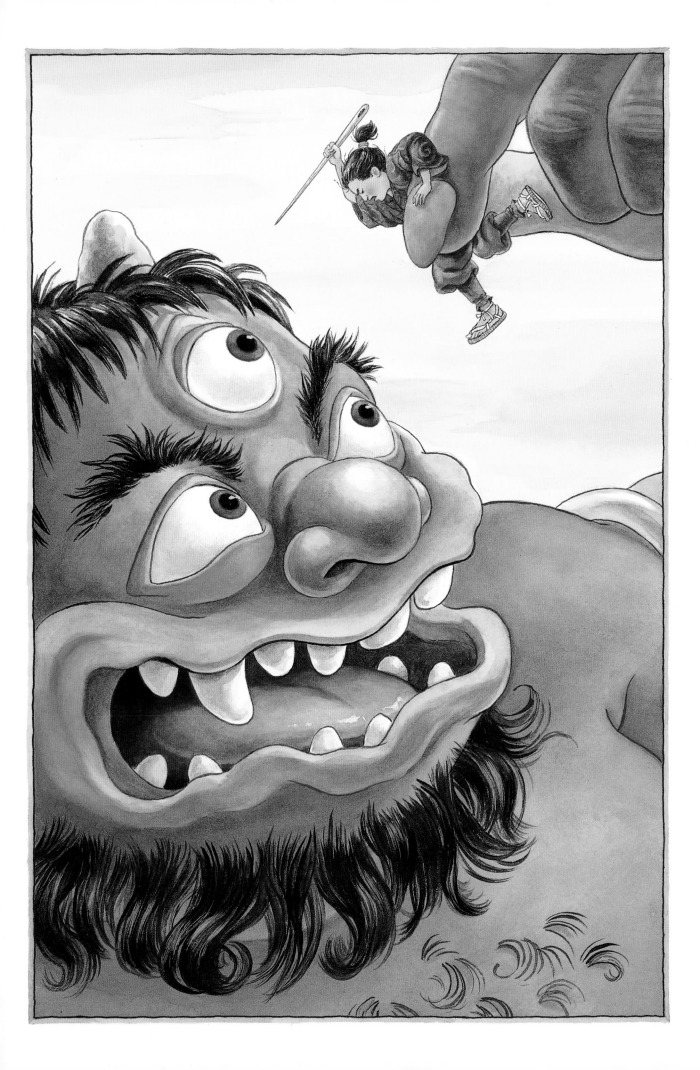

"Then I must wish for both of us!" Plum Blossom
struggled to lift the huge mallet off the ground and let
it fall again.

As she did so the ground shook. The wind blew and the sky grew dark. They both cried out and covered their eyes in fear.

When they dared to look again, Little Fingerling had vanished. In his place stood a handsome samurai warrior. The hollow rice straw was now a magnificently carved scabbard and the needle his mother had given him had become a samurai sword.

Together the couple walked on to the temple of Kanzeon to thank her for their good fortune. When they returned home, Issun Boshi humbly asked her father for Plum Blossom's hand in marriage.

The nobleman embraced him. "You have always shown yourself to be brave, noble and resourceful. Now at last you appear as you were inwardly."

So Issun Boshi and Plum Blossom lived happily in Kyoto for the rest of their lives; and Issun Boshi, now no longer Little Fingerling, brought his parents from their farm so that he might care for them honourably in their old age.